Puffin Books

Editor : Kaye Webb

Emily's Voyage

Emily was a Guinea-pig who was very fond of cooking and housework. She got up early every day, and all day long she was busy polishing and ironing, beating mats and stirring puddings.

But Emily also loved to travel, and every so often her house went suddenly dull for her. The walls seemed too close together, and the sound of the kettle was no consolation. Then she lifted her nose, and sniffed the winds from far-off places. Beneath her she seemed to feel the pitch and toss of a deck, and instead of the twitter of sparrows, she heard the wild cry of the gulls.

There was only one way to cure a feeling like that – to give way to it. A friendly Weasel made all the arrangements, and in no time at all Emily was packed up ready to go. She sat on the sofa in the parlour, and her bag stood ready at her feet. She wore goloshes and a thick plaid overcoat with a cape, and her hat was tied on to her head with a woollen scarf.

Very soon now the two Brown Owls would come to escort her to her ship, the strangest craft you ever saw, bound for an unknown destination and the queerest adventures, with only a poetical Hare as Captain and a bunch of frightened rabbits for crew . . .

JASON CLIFT

Emma Smith

Emily's Voyage

Illustrated by Margaret Gordon

Penguin Books

Penguin Books Ltd, Harmondsworth,
Middlesex, England
Penguin Books Australia Ltd, Ringwood,
Victoria, Australia

First published by Macmillan 1966
Published in Puffin Books 1971
Reprinted 1972
Copyright © Emma Smith, 1966

Made and printed in Great Britain by
Cox & Wyman Ltd,
London, Reading and Fakenham
Set in Monotype Baskerville

Chapter One

Emily was a Guinea-pig who was very fond of cooking and housework. She lived with her brother Arthur, and looked after him well, so that he was never hungry, and never had holes in the heels of his socks. She got up early every day, and all day long she was busy, and hardly had time to enjoy the view from the window, except when she shook a duster, or called her brother in for lunch.

Arthur attended to the garden, and culti-vated flowers and vegetables. He was not very energetic, but his cabbages were the best in the district. He loved his garden quite as much as Emily loved her house. But while his sister was always hurrying about from one room to another, polishing and ironing, beating mats and stirring puddings, Arthur was happiest when he was sitting still on a flower-pot, doing absolutely nothing. He said that a garden should be given plenty of attention, but not interfered with.

Arthur never wanted to go away. But Emily did. For Emily was a Guinea-pig who loved to travel, and every so often – once, or it might be twice a year – her house went suddenly dull for her. The walls seemed too close together, and the sound of the kettle was no consolation. Then she lifted her nose, and sniffed the winds from far-off places.

'Do you know,' she said to Arthur one day, 'I've never seen a volcano.'

Arthur was bending over to tie some Michaelmas daisies to a stick; he only grunted.

Emily went back into the parlour and tried to get on with her dusting, but the duster flew so wildly here and there, like a flag fluttering

at the mast-head of a ship in a storm, that she broke her best china candlestick. She went upstairs with the duster in her paw, and sat at her bedroom window, staring out. Beneath her she seemed to feel the pitch and toss of a deck, and instead of the twitter of sparrows, she heard the wild cry of the gulls.

Arthur finished tying up his daisies. When he straightened himself and took a step back he bumped into someone. Turning round, he discovered the Weasel.

'Oh, hullo!' said Arthur, rubbing his paw

on his trousers to get off the dirt, 'I'm glad you're here. You're just who's wanted. Emily's got one of her moods come on. She goes right off the cooking when one of her moods come on. I haven't had a proper meal for days. She gave me turnips for tea yesterday.'

'Nothing wrong with turnips,' said the Weasel, gently.

'She forgot to cook 'em,' said Arthur.

The Weasel went silently into the house and looked in the parlour, but no one was there. The kitchen was empty as well, and instead of a fire in the stove there were only ashes. He went into the garden again and looked up at Emily's bedroom, and sure enough, there she was. He whistled. Emily opened her window at once, and leaned out.

'Time you was off, it sounds to me,' said the Weasel. 'How about it?'

Emily raised her head and studied the

sky for a moment. Then she closed her window and came downstairs to talk it over with the Weasel.

They paced the soggy grass together, up and down, while Arthur scratched away in a corner with a rake; for the summer was over – it was autumn now – and he was making a bonfire.

'Any special place you had in mind?' the Weasel said.

Emily was silent.

'The sea?' he asked her.

She looked at him, and her little eyes shone; she threw up her head and planted her legs firmly, and a great gust of wind swooped across the garden, and lifted the dead leaves in a cloud all round them, and scattered Arthur's bonfire, and blew out the match in his hand, which vexed him very much indeed.

'Mind you, it isn't the best time of year for sailing,' said the Weasel, and as he spoke a few drops of rain fell from the low clouds above – 'but if you put it off, you're liable to lose the feeling – the best time for going is when you happen to want to go.'

Emily said she was ready to leave as soon as her bag was packed.

They took another turn about the garden. The morning grew darker and darker. Yellow smoke came pouring out of the top of Arthur's bonfire, and then the rain began in earnest. It fell from the sky like water from a bucket. As Emily hurried to the shelter of her porch, the Weasel turned up his collar and pulled his hat down over his eyes and sprang away over the wall.

'But what shall I do for a boat?' she cried after him. 'How shall I get there? Where shall I go?'

She thought she heard him call – 'Leave it to me' – but the sound of the rain was too loud for her to be sure.

Arthur came stamping up with a sack on his head. 'I can't get it to burn at all,' he said, crossly. 'First it's the wind, then it's the rain –' His bonfire was a failure.

'Arthur,' said Emily, rather anxiously, 'you won't mind if I take a little sea-voyage, will you?'

'Good gracious me, no!' said Arthur, cheering up at once. 'How long do you mean to be away?'

'Oh, not very long,' said Emily, vaguely, and she went upstairs to pack.

Chapter Two

By half past five Emily had made her arrangements. She sat on the sofa in the parlour, and her bag, bulging with all things necessary to a traveller, stood ready at her feet. Her green umbrella was propped by her side. She wore goloshes and a thick plaid overcoat, with a cape, and her hat was tied on to her head with a woollen scarf.

'Now Arthur, do pay attention – there's plenty of food in the house, and Carrie will come in every day to cook and clean, but be sure to light the stove in good time so that the oven can heat. And don't forget to take your boots off before you come into the house, and remember to turn off the taps at night, and put the guard in front of the fire, and lock the

door, and wind the clock – Arthur, do stop fidgeting.'

'I've got to fidget about a bit so as not to go to sleep,' said Arthur.

Just before seven o'clock there was a bumping sound outside the front door, followed by a light rustling or scratching that might have been tapping. When she opened the door, Emily found her porch entirely filled by two large Brown Owls, standing side by side and silent. One of them held a piece of folded paper in his beak. She took it, and unfolded it, and read what was written on the paper. This is what she read:

'Schooner sailing at midnight. Passage booked. Air transport arranged for one Guinea-pig, one bag.'

The message was unsigned.

Emily had not travelled by carrier-Owl before, but she knew what it meant: Owls have no consideration for their passengers, and if they happen to drop one, never stop to pick him up. Many animals think it far too dangerous a way of getting about. Emily was not put off by danger, but she did prefer, when taking a risk, to be comfortable, and so looked for a seat; but there was no seat – nothing to sit on.

'I'm not a parcel,' she said to the nearest Owl. 'You can't pick me up by my string, you know.'

The Brown Owl stared over the top of

14

Emily's head. He only moved his great claws and slightly fluffed his feathers.

Arthur leaned forward and whispered: 'You'd better be off, my dear – they don't want to stand about –'

'I'm ready,' said Emily.

She embraced her brother. He disappeared for a moment inside the folds of her plaid overcoat. Then she opened her large green umbrella, and turning it upside down, so that it became a sort of boat, stepped aboard. The handle stuck up like a mast, and she gripped it firmly.

'Arthur, listen – I meant to tell you – there's any amount of black-currant syrup in case you get a cough. Oh, wait – !' she cried.

But the Brown Owls had waited long enough. There was a sudden commotion of feathers, and in a hurly-burly of beating wings and swirling darkness, Emily felt her umbrella and herself to be snatched violently

upwards. It was a giddy moment. She closed her eyes.

When she opened them she knew they must be high above the trees, but she could see nothing, not even a star. She was being carried steadily forward. All round her the night was black; the cold air rushed against her. She could feel and hear the continual sweep of wings, close above; and then the Brown Owl hooted – and from somewhere behind came the answering hoot of the other Brown Owl, following.

Emily remained standing upright at her post. She was afraid to sit down in case she upset herself over the side as she did so. In spite of the cold, she grew more and more sleepy.

'I must not go to sleep,' she told herself. 'If I drop off,' she thought, 'I'm bound to drop off.'

So she fixed her thoughts on Arthur, for when she thought of Arthur, she worried and worry kept her awake.

'If only I had had time to tell him where the syrup is – if only he keeps his chest covered, he won't get a cough – if only he doesn't get a cough, he won't need the syrup –'

Arthur too was sorry not to have learnt the whereabouts of the syrup. Those Brown Owls had disconcerted him a good deal, and now they were gone he felt the need of fortification. He searched the house, but in vain: he could find no syrup, and was obliged to eat a couple of pots of raspberry jam instead. He ate it with a spoon, which Arthur thought the best way to eat jam, though he seldom got the chance – Emily only allowed him to eat it on bread. Then he ate a large currant cake, without troubling to slice it up first. And then, covered in crumbs, he put his feet on the mantelpiece, and lay back in his chair, smiling, and went to sleep. Presently the clock stopped ticking. The front door rattled softly. Arthur began to snore.

In the meantime, miles away, Emily's flight was ending. The umbrella tilted over, and the Brown Owl began to circle down. And as he glided lower, he uttered again his melancholy hoot; and from behind, invisible in the darkness, the other Brown Owl hooted too.

The ferrule of Emily's umbrella scraped against stone, dragged a little way, and stopped. Emily stepped out on to a stone jetty. A moment after, her bag came down with a thump at her feet, and the second Brown Owl shuffled into place alongside the first.

Emily closed her umbrella and peered about her. She could hear the slap-slap of water somewhere close, and smell the saltiness of the air, but it was hard to see anything. Only one lamp shone feebly. The jetty seemed deserted. But just then she caught the sound of whistling, and from a dim pile of baskets and crates, a figure appeared. Emily recognized the Weasel.

'I don't see a schooner,' she called across to him. She was tired, and the shadows confused her.

'Schooner's not far – you settle your fare and make haste,' he said, and added warningly: 'Tide's on the turn.'

So Emily got out her purse, and from it the necessary money. But before paying she wrote a few words on a piece of paper. This is what she wrote:

'Syrup under Preserving Pan'

'I would be so much obliged if you would take this message to my brother,' she said

The nearest Owl snapped the paper up in his beak. His claw closed over the money.

'Arthur's all right,' said the Weasel, with a grin. 'No need to fret yourself on his account.'

'Good night!' called Emily.

But the Brown Owls were gone at once, without a word of farewell, only a rustle of feathers and a disturbance of the cold night air.

Emily stared up. 'They might have said good-bye – at *least* good-bye –'

'Come on, or you'll miss your passage,' said the Weasel. 'It's no good expecting conversation from an Owl.'

Emily followed him down some slippery steps and at the bottom lay a dinghy, bobbing on the water. She took the Weasel's paw to steady herself, and the moment she was embarked, he began to row. Emily looked over her shoulder and saw the single jetty light recede. Then she looked ahead. A large shape was looming out of the darkness: it

was the schooner. The Weasel shipped his oars and stood up.

'Hullo there! – Mate ahoy! Passenger coming aboard.'

A rope ladder dangled in front of Emily's nose.

'Up you go,' said the Weasel. 'I'll see about the bag. Make haste,' he said again.

Step by step Emily climbed the dark side

of the ship to the deck above. It was not easy to have to go up a rope ladder for the first time in pitch black night, with a large umbrella hooked over one arm, but Emily did her best: travellers have to be intrepid. As soon as she stepped aboard, she felt herself seized by a number of paws; a babel of voices surrounded her:

'This way – passenger this way – passenger to be kept off deck – passenger to stay in cabin –'

'I'll do as I please,' said Emily, attempting to shake herself free. 'Leave me alone,' she cried, indignantly. 'How dare you! Who are you? I am a traveller – I won't be shoved –'

But although she tried to resist, her heels would slip, and so she was tugged and pushed across the deck, and down a stairway, and in at a door; and the door was slammed behind her.

A second later, it flew open, and her bag

came hurtling in. Then, slam! – it was shut again.

Emily was affronted, and out of breath. Her clothes were disarranged. What a way to be treated! She meant to find the Captain at once, and complain. But all of a sudden, while she was still straightening her hat, pandemonium broke out overhead.

'Goodness,' she thought, listening in wonder, 'whatever can be happening?'

Footsteps were pattering to and fro. She could hear shouts, cries, the sound of hammering, a creaking and a scraping, the clankety rattle of a chain. Then came a tremendous thud directly above her, and Emily changed her mind: it was not the right time to go in search of the Captain. She took off her scarf and her hat and her overcoat and her goloshes and looked round at her cabin instead.

It was a very small cabin. It contained a

bunk and a porthole and a hurricane lantern suspended from a hook; nothing else. But it did not seem to Emily bare. It seemed to her, in the yellowy light of the lantern, a cosy place. The flame burned steadily; the shadows scarcely flickered. After the hazards of her journey, it was a haven – secure and tranquil, like home – and her feelings were comforted.

She opened her bag and got out her blanket and her diary. Then she climbed on the bunk, and wrapped herself snug in her blanket, and took the red elastic band off her diary, and began to write. Her writing was tidy and clear. This is what Emily wrote:

'Came away from Home tonight by Carrier-Owl – my first flight – most exhilarating. Schooner sails with Tide. Crew not Accustomed to Passengers – no manners – most regrettable. Memo: must ask what Port we sail for, also what cargo we carry –'

Here she stopped writing and thought of the Weasel. She wondered if he were safely back on shore again. She thought of Arthur, and his chest, and the syrup, and of whether he had wound the clock and locked the door – at this moment, the ship gave a lurch. The hurricane lantern jerked and swung. Emily snatched up her pencil.

'I am at SEA' she wrote.

And her wobbly writing proved it to be true.

Chapter Three

The first thing Emily did when she opened her eyes in the morning was to look through the little round porthole, and there, no more than an inch or so away, was water – the great green ocean itself, right up against her window. Only glass separated her from all the sea of the world.

Emily clambered down from her bunk. The floor was moving. It tilted over. Very much surprised, she found herself running across the cabin – she had not meant to do so. When she turned round, the floor had tilted the other way, and she found herself running quickly back.

'Just as though I were on wheels,' she thought, 'and without a brake, either.'

Her bag, too, was sliding and bumping about. She remembered all her possessions inside it – supposing they were to be damaged? – her painting equipment, her kettle and teapot and spirit-stove; her mug and her own hurricane lantern; her sewing-case, her first-aid outfit, her change of under-clothes. If the bottle of meths got broken, or the bottle of sal volatile, she would never be able to make herself tea, or bring herself round from a fainting fit.

Emily managed to heave the bag up on her bunk, and wedge it with the blanket. Then she tied her hat on firmly, and made sure all her buttons were done up. It was certainly very difficult to keep her balance: nothing stayed still, not even her own feet.

Emily climbed the companionway, and cautiously put her head outside. The wind was a terrific surprise – it tore at her hat and scarf.

'Goodness, how strong!' said Emily.

Her eyes were stung by the salt of flying spray. She wondered if she ought to go on deck; it might not be safe. And she waited, hoping for a lull, but the wind blew and blew, without a pause. So, reminding herself that she was a traveller and that travellers sometimes have to take a risk, Emily ventured out.

At first it seemed as if she were alone, surrounded by miles of white-speckled sea, under a billowing cloud of white sails. The ship flew on like a bird going home, like a ship in a dream. But could she really be the only soul aboard? Then she observed a solitary figure leaning on a rail in the bows of the schooner – probably another passenger, Emily thought, and was pleased at the prospect of company and conversation during the voyage ahead. Perhaps he too sketched in water-colours? She decided to introduce herself.

As she edged her way forward, step by step, Emily perceived that the stranger was a Hare. He wore a navy-blue seafaring coat, and a purple neckerchief. His long legs were carelessly crossed.

'Good morning!' she shouted.

The Hare paid her no attention. She touched his arm; he started and turned. His whiskers were tangled by the wind; his ears streamed away. Emily thought his appearance most unusual and interesting.

'I wonder if you could direct me, please, to the breakfast parlour –'

He put one paw on his chest; the other he flung out across the water, towards the far horizon.

'I am a Hare!' he cried, with flashing eyes.

What a curious way to answer! Emily thought perhaps she had better ask somebody else.

Only where was the Captain? she wondered, battling her way back again. Where was the crew? All those persons who had pushed her so rudely last night – where were they? At least there must be someone steering – and sure enough, inside the wheelhouse, out of the wind, she found a very small Water Rat. He stood on a box to steer.

'Hullo!' he said. 'I've been watching you – just as well you made sure to hold on so tight.'

'And supposing I hadn't?' she asked him.

'With them skirts and a following wind, I reckon you'd have taken off – gone up, just like a kite, if you'd have let go,' said the Water Rat. There was a tinge of regret in his voice.

Emily was thankful she had held on tightly. But was it really so easy for a passenger to blow away? She felt a sudden pang for home, where only such things as leaves, or hats, got blown away, and creatures were safe.

'I should like a cup of tea,' she said; for her sinking spirits might well be due to an empty stomach, and tea would give her courage again.

The Water Rat put out one paw and pulled a chain. Emily could hear a bell clanging, somewhere below, but no one responded to the summons. The Water Rat pulled again, and went on pulling until at last a Rabbit tottered into the wheelhouse and sank to the floor with a groan.

'What is it?' cried Emily, in consternation. 'Are you hurt?'

'I wish I never come,' she heard him mutter. 'I feel *that* seedy.'

'Seedy?' she asked.

'Sick, he means,' said the Water Rat. 'They're all sick, the whole lot of 'em – always are. Here you, pull yourself together – passenger wants a cup of tea. You nip along and get her one, and a couple of ship's biscuits too. Anything else you fancy?' he said to Emily.

She answered that tea and biscuits would suit her admirably. The Rabbit staggered off.

'Do you mean that *all* the crew are suffering from sea-sickness?' Emily asked.

'Every one of 'em,' said the Water Rat.

'Rabbits turn sick very easy. They didn't ever ought to come to sea – it's not in their nature. I've told 'em so, many a time, but it makes no difference – they will come.'

'But surely,' said Emily, 'the crew isn't only Rabbits?' Her opinion of Rabbits had always been low – she thought them un-resourceful.

'Every one of 'em,' he said again. 'The Skipper always signs on Rabbits – don't ask me why. Never any other sort of animal – except for me, that is – I'm an exception, and just as well I am. Me an' you are the only creatures aboard this ship as isn't Rabbits – and the Skipper himself, of course.'

'The Skipper?' asked Emily, and her heart sank anxiously lower.

'Him you've been having a chat with, up in the bows,' said the Water Rat.

Emily was dismayed. She might have admired the tall Hare as a passenger, but he

34

did not seem to her to look at all as a Captain should. And surely the Water Rat was too small and far too young to be left in charge of the schooner? She said to him:

'Aren't you a little young for steering?'

'You might as well say as I'm a little young for breathing,' said the Water Rat. 'Age don't signify when it come to boats – what counts is what you're used to. Now I'm used to water, and a Rabbit – he's not.'

'I'm not either,' said Emily, feeling she must admit it. 'This is my first sea-voyage.'

'Oh, you'll do well enough, I daresay,' he answered, with a sideways glance. 'Some pick it up quicker than others. You've got quite a look of the sea about you.'

The Water Rat was young, to be sure, thought Emily, but very sensible. She began to feel more confidence in him.

'Rabbits,' he went on, 'never do pick it up.

I'm down in the ship's papers as Cabin-boy, but I'll tell you what I am *in fact* – I'm the First Mate of this schooner, and the Bo'sun, and the Second Mate, and the crew. Come to that,' he said to Emily, grinning, 'I'm the Skipper too. I run away from the river three trips back. It wasn't the river I minded, it was the banks – they was too close. I don't like to feel limited. One day I'm going to have a ship of my own.'

At this moment the Rabbit reappeared, dumped a billy-can full of tea, and a pile of biscuits, in front of Emily, and bolted off.

'Look where you're going, can't you?' roared the Captain, who was just then stooping to come in at the wheelhouse door. He heaved the Rabbit aside by the scruff of his neck.

'No brains, those fellows. Never think of anyone else. Ah ha! – tea! Splendid! – just what I was wanting.'

He picked up the billy-can and drank it
dry. A little steam was all that was left of
Emily's tea.

'Not enough sugar,' said the Captain. He
dabbed his whiskers with a silk handkerchief
and clapped the Water Rat round the

shoulders. 'Stick to it, young 'un – we'll make a seaman of you yet.'

'Yessir!' said the Water Rat.

The Captain turned to Emily. 'So we meet again – Miss Emily Guinea-Pig, I believe?'

Emily gave him her paw. Her manner was reserved. Since he had drunk her tea, she thought him a good deal less handsome.

'You are comfortable, I trust?' he said. 'My crew are seeing to your needs? Ask for whatever you want.'

He stared out of the wheelhouse, humming a tune.

Emily remembered the note in her diary. 'I should be glad if you could tell me where we are bound for – what port?' she said.

The Captain spun round. 'Destination unknown!' he cried.

Emily was shocked. 'Do you really mean you don't know where we are going?'

'I haven't the least idea,' said the Captain.

'I leave it to chance – to the wind, you know.'

'I think that most unwise,' said Emily, and out of the corner of her eye she saw the Water Rat's grin.

'I am a poet, Miss Pig,' said the Captain. 'I have a poet's feelings.' He bowed, with an air of disappointment, and went away.

Emily thought it very rude of him to call her Pig. She was sure he had only said her name wrong so as to vex her, and she was vexed; she was also very hungry. But the biscuits were soggy with spilt tea. Emily picked up the billy-can.

'I am going to find the kitchen – the galley, I think you call it – and I am going to get us something for breakfast. Because it seems to me that if I don't, we shall both of us starve.'

'That's the spirit,' cried the Water Rat, nodding at her gleefully. 'We're going to get along fine – you an' me an' this old ship.'

'I think perhaps,' said Emily, 'you had better teach me how to steer. Poet indeed!' she added, with a sniff.

Chapter Four

The galley was in some disorder, and deserted. But the stove was alight, and there were plenty of provisions. Emily was getting her sea-legs: she was beginning to be able to balance herself to the rise and fall of the ship. She made porridge and tea, and carried it up to the wheelhouse. The Captain was nowhere to be seen.

'In his cabin, I daresay,' said the Water Rat. 'He's mostly in his cabin. Comes up for a breather now and again.'

After breakfast, Emily asked if she might be allowed to steer for a while.

'You try it, and welcome,' said the Water Rat, obligingly stepping off his box.

Emily took hold of the spokes of the wheel.

And at once, it seemed to her, she became a part of the ship. She could feel the pitch and toss of it deep inside her, like the beat of her own heart. And she could feel more, something huge beyond the ship – the sea itself; the mysterious push of its great waves, the pull of its tides. By the time Emily had finished her spell of steering, she was a different animal: not a passenger any more, but a sailor.

She went below and tidied the galley.

Then she set off to find the missing crew, and presently discovered their quarters, deep down in the hold of the ship. It was not at all a nice place, Emily thought – dark and stuffy, and crowded with hammocks. She brought the Rabbits mugs of tea, and did what she could for them with dabs of lavender water and encouraging conversation. But they only groaned, and one of them asked her to go away.

Emily was much puzzled by a sound of

tapping. It came from beyond the far bulwark.

'What is there,' she asked, 'on the other side of that wall?' There was no door through it.

One of the Rabbits muttered: 'Cargo.'

'But surely the cargo isn't alive?'

Tap, tap, tap, she heard again.

'That noise is a live noise,' said Emily.

She went up to the wheelhouse and told the Water Rat:

'There's someone tapping in the cargo.'

They looked at each other, silently speculating: who?

'It'll take the two of us to get that hatch-cover off,' said the Water Rat, eventually. 'Tell you what we'll do – we'll lash the wheel. Wind's holding nice and steady – she'll steer herself.'

He lashed the wheel, and the schooner steered herself, while they untied the stiff strings of a tarpaulin and shoved back the lid of the hatch. Then the Water Rat fetched a hurricane lantern, and together they leaned over the side of the big black hole.

'Anyone there?' called the Water Rat, and his voice went echoing down.

The ship heeled over. Emily lost her balance and fell against the Water Rat. The lantern was jerked from his paw, and dropped like a stone. They heard the smash of glass, far below, and saw the horrifying flames shoot

up. But someone was there. They glimpsed a figure. There was a scuffling sound, and the flames were extinguished. In the succeeding darkness, someone very nimble was shinning up the ladder towards them, and a moment later they saw: it was the Weasel.

'Well, I never!' thought Emily, astonished and glad.

He gave her a nod as he swung himself over the edge of the hatch, and she thought he was whistling, only the wind was whistling louder. They tugged the hatch-cover into place and tied the tarpaulin, and then, without a word spoken, struggled back, all three, to the shelter of the wheelhouse.

'You're a stowaway!' burst out the Water Rat, very excited and respectful.

'Call it what you like,' said the Weasel. He spoke softly, but his eyes were sharp as needles. 'I reckoned I might be needed.'

'I'm very glad you're here,' said Emily.

'Ah well, I reckoned you might be,' said the Weasel. 'As for you, son,' he said and his narrow look transfixed the Water Rat, 'you be more careful – that ain't the sort of cargo for you to go dropping lamps on.'

'I don't happen to know what our cargo is, this trip,' said the Water Rat, uncomfortably.

'Then I'll tell you,' said the Weasel. 'It's fireworks. Funny sort of cargo, that seems to me. And safety-pins – boxes and boxes of 'em. Thousands of safety-pins. Whatever was your Skipper thinking of to ship a cargo of safety-pins and fireworks?'

'He always calculates to carry a cargo anyone might want,' said the Water Rat, 'on
account of not knowing what part of the
world we may be going to end up in, see.'

The Weasel shook his head disapprovingly.
'That's the way to travel on land,' he said.
'But water's different. You can take your time
on land, take any direction, start off when you
like, stop when you like, and never mind
where you're going till you get there. But
when you go to sea, you've got to have clear
intentions. Land waits for you; water don't –
it's on the move as well, that's why. What you
need for sailing,' said the Weasel, 'is
navigation.'

'Yessir!' cried the Water Rat, enthusiasti-
cally. 'Right you are, sir! Navigation it is!'

The Weasel regarded him more favourably.
'Did they call you anything special, back
where you come from?'

'Tiffy, sir.'

'Well then, Tiffy, what you and me are going to do is, we're going to plot a course.'

'Yessir!' said the Water Rat, once again.

Emily was told to take the wheel and to steer a little south of sou'sou'west. The other two unfolded charts and spread them out, and began to discuss currents, and soundings, and reefs, and equinox.

Some hours later, towards the end of the afternoon, the door was flung open and the Captain appeared, tall and wild against the darkening sky. Papers and charts, skirts, coats, the Captain's ears – everything flapped in a whirl of wind, till the door banged shut.

'Ah ha! – so that's where you are,' he said to Emily, shaking the spray from his collar. The drips flew off in Emily's face. 'I was beginning to think you'd been washed over-board – I couldn't find you anywhere. Passengers aren't allowed in the wheelhouse, you know. It's against the rules.'

'Bother the rules,' said Emily, sharply. She had been steering a long time, and was tired.

The Captain seemed delighted. 'You're quite right, Miss Thingummy-Pig,' he cried. 'Bother the rules! – make 'em and break 'em! What's the use of a rule except to break it – eh?'

This was not Emily's opinion at all: she thought good rules were very important indeed, and should never be broken; only bad ones.

'You misunderstand me, Captain – '

But the Captain had taken hold of her arm.

'Leave that wheel,' he said, impatiently. 'I want you to hear my new poem – been at it all day. Come along, we'll go down to my cabin – it's more comfortable there – you'll be able to listen properly.'

'I can't come along,' said Emily, giving her arm an angry twitch. 'My name,' she said, 'is Emily Guinea-Pig, and I'm steering.'

The Captain looked surprised. 'Well, somebody else can steer – get one of the fellows to do it.'

He glanced about, and his eye fell on the Weasel.

'Who's this?' he said, with a frown.

'Member of the crew, sir – just joined up – acting First Mate,' said the Water Rat, smartly, saluting as he spoke.

'Ah!' said the Captain, vaguely. 'Glad to have you with us.' He leaned forward and peered at the Weasel. 'Haven't I seen you before sometime? – booking a passage? – yesterday, was it?'

'Might have been,' said the Weasel, staring back at him. 'Could have done – it's a small world – yesterday's a long way off.' Very softly, still staring, he began to whistle.

'So it is!' said the Captain. 'Over and done with – I've never cared for the past myself – what's gone is always dull. But today! – ah!

– tomorrow! – who knows what may be going to happen? – anything at all! You'd like to hear my poem,' he said to the Weasel. 'You'd appreciate it.'

He closed his eyes and threw out one paw, as Emily recalled him doing at their first meeting, and in a loud voice recited the following stanzas:

> '*I am a Hare!*
> *I do! I dare!*
> *Let go! Let go!*
> *You ask me where?*
> *I do not know.*
> *Or fast, or slow —*
> *I do not care*
> *I do! I dare!*
> *I am a Hare!*
> *The sea below —*
> *Above — the air.*
> *I am a Hare!*
> *Blow, tempest, blow!*'

'Well?' said the Captain, stopping and looking round.

Emily was silent. She considered that poetry, like painting, should be accurate, and this poem seemed to her to be not altogether true. He was a Hare – but did he dare? And as for doing, she had never seen him doing anything.

'Well?' said the Captain, again.

'Not enough,' said the Weasel.

'You think it's too short? You're right! – I'll make it longer.'

With a rush of wind and a bang of the door, the Captain disappeared.

'We'll do better without him,' said the Weasel. 'It's your turn at the wheel, young Tiffy – sou'sou'west – and time for cocoa, I reckon. No – I'll fetch it,' he said, for Emily, having sunk down exhausted was attempting to struggle up again. 'Cocoa with a drop of rum in it, that's what you need. There's nothing like rum to pull you round – unless it's more rum. You done very well for a learner.'

'Rum?' she queried, faintly.

'You'll like it,' said the Weasel.

Chapter Five

For seven days and seven nights they sailed south, and the air grew warmer and the sea more blue, and the great gale that had blown them along so boisterously dropped to a pleasant breeze. The crew recovered from their sickness and lay all over the hot decks, playing cards and snoozing. The Captain continued to write poetry in his cabin, or stood for hours in the bows, gazing ahead at the far horizon. Emily and the Weasel and Tiffy the Water Rat between them steered and cooked and plotted the course. It was a happy time. They were all very well contented.

Emily thought of Arthur quite often, but not anxiously any more; rather as though he were in one dream, and she in another. The sparkle of sea by day, and the sparkle of stars by night, lulled and entranced her, and she felt that nothing could ever go wrong, or change.

But on the eighth day the weather went wrong, and everything changed with it.

Just as the sun was sinking, the Captain rushed pell-mell into the wheelhouse.

'Land!' he shouted, and his eyes blazed with excitement. 'Coming up over the horizon – land!'

'That's not land,' said the Weasel, sharply. 'That's clouds. And I don't like 'em – they're coming up a sight too fast. Tiffy!'

'Yessir!'

'Hark at the wind.'

'It's making a different sort of noise,' said the Water Rat, his ears pricked.

'Take a sniff outside.'

'It's blowing stronger.'

'We're in for a storm, and a nasty one too,

and if we don't get those sails down in double quick time we'll all be blown to the other side of nowhere,' said the Weasel. 'Where's the crew?'

But the decks were deserted. The crew, alarmed by ominous signs, had already taken to their bunks. The Captain too had vanished. Only the Weasel and Tiffy remained to get down the sails as best they could, while Emily stood at the wheel, and darkness fell fast, and the sound of the wind grew louder and louder as the storm approached, and the water beneath began to churn and heave.

Then for a moment the wind stopped blowing and the sea stopped heaving. In the pitch black of night the ship stood still, and there was silence. A moment after, with a flash of lightning and a crash of thunder, the storm struck them, and the sea boiled up, and the wind came screaming into the rigging.

That was a terrible night. Rain fell in torrents. There were no stars, no moon. Huge waves poured over the decks, and in every flash of lightning they could see the torn canvas of the sails they had failed to get stowed in time, streaming out in black ribbons from the tossing masts.

And high above in the ragged clouds, marvellous colours exploded, blossomed and faded, like flowers of the storm, for the Captain had broken open a crate of cargo and was letting off rockets by the dozen.

'Help!' he muttered. 'This is a signal – here's another – S.O.S., ship in distress – S.O.S., we're in a mess – '

No help came, but instead, loud above the roaring of the tempest, the crack of breaking timber. The Captain threw aside his box of matches and burst into the wheelhouse, where the Weasel and Emily and Tiffy the Water Rat clung with all their strength to the kicking wheel, and tried to steer a course.

'Abandon ship!' he cried.

'What was it, Tiffy? – take a look.'

'Mast gone amidships, sir.'

The schooner shuddered; the wheel spun round in their paws.

'Rudder away!' cried the Water Rat, and let go of the wheel; for it was no use trying to steer any more. Without a rudder the ship turned in circles, like a piece of driftwood.

The Captain buried his head in his paws. 'Going down, the lot of us! Going down – the Captain too!'

All night long to steady his nerves they dosed him with swigs of rum from the Weasel's bottle; and although Emily would much have preferred a cup of tea, she had a drop or two as well – it was better than nothing. Tiffy produced a mouth-organ.

'Come on, Skipper – give us a song.'

'What, *sing?* – with the ship going down?'

'Why not?' said the Weasel.

So they stamped their feet, and passed the bottle, and sang, greatly increasing the terror of the Rabbits down below. And at every seventh wave the Captain started up with the same despairing cry:

'Abandon ship!'

When morning came they were still afloat. They stood at the rail in that fierce dawn, straining their eyes to see whatever they could; and what they saw was white surf and tossing spray, directly ahead.

'Rocks!' cried the Captain. 'We'll smash to pieces!'

But the Weasel was staring at something beyond the rocks, at a faint grey shape, scarcely visible through the driving rain.

'That's land, that is,' he said. 'It's an island – I can see palm-trees. Lower the boats.'

'Lower the boats!' the Captain yelled.

'There's no boats left to lower,' Tiffy answered. 'Washed away, sir.'

'Drat that crew,' said the Weasel. 'Can't they even tie knots? Then throw out the anchors, Tiff – if the anchors hold, there's still a chance – '

'Aye aye, sir.'

Emily went below to fetch up her bag and umbrella, and also the crew; they had to be got on deck somehow – they were certainly doomed if they stayed where they were.

'Come along at once,' she called. 'There's no time to lose. We're quite close to a nice island.'

The crew hastened to obey her, recoiling in dread at the terrible sight that met their eyes.

Tiffy and the Weasel had heaved the anchors overboard; their chains came rattling up from the chain-lockers, and down, down, into the sea, and clean out of sight.

'Anchors all gone, sir,' Tiffy reported.

'Sorry to have to say, they wasn't fastened at the end.'

The schooner drifted rapidly on. The noise of surf was deafening, and the rocks, rushing nearer, looked as sharp as knives. Emily was much afraid.

'Only,' she thought, 'I mustn't let the others see I am. I do wish Arthur was here – but oh! I'm glad he's not –'

At that moment she heard the Weasel shout:

'Hold tight!'

Emily held as tight as she could.

Chapter Six

The schooner drove on towards disaster, and no one could stop it. Into the foaming surf it plunged, and then, with a splintering crash, the voyage was over, and the ship was a wreck, and the wreck was stuck fast on the rocks, battered by waves, surrounded by the devastating sea. Not far off was a sandy beach.

'So close,' the Weasel muttered, 'and we can't get there.'

'I can!' said the Water Rat, saluting. 'I'll swim ashore with a line, sir. I'm a swimmer – only one aboard.'

'What we want's a flyer, not a swimmer,' said the Weasel. 'You'd never do it, Tiffy.'

'I'm a very good swimmer, sir.'

'All right then – you have a go, and the best of luck.'

They poured the last of the rum down his throat, and tied a double cotton-line round his stomach, and watched him spring clear of the wrecked vessel and disappear beneath the turbulent water, as though for ever. The crew and the Captain raised a cheer, but the Weasel was silent, and so was Emily. She clutched the rail and felt her heart beat faster, with painful bangs. Supposing they never saw young Tiffy alive again?

'There he is!' said the Weasel.

The brown head of the Water Rat showed for an instant, and was swamped by another wave. It bobbed up again nearer the shore, and was gone. They waited and waited: not a sign of him. Then the Water Rat was lifted high on a colossal breaker and, like a piece of flotsam, flung up the beach.

'He's dead, poor chap,' said the Captain.

'Dead be blowed!' said the Weasel.

'He's saved us!' said Emily.

And so he had. They saw him sit up and shake himself, and heard him yell:

'I *done* it! – I knew I could!'

They rigged the cotton-line from ship to shore, tying it round a mast at one end, and round a palm tree at the other. Some kind of conveyance was needed to get them over; Emily suggested her large green umbrella. But when this had been opened and turned upside down and slung from a shackle, the Captain looked uneasy, and the crew appalled. They refused to trust themselves to a green umbrella.

'It's really quite dependable for travelling in,' Emily assured them, 'as long as you keep still, and keep calm, and hold on. I'll show you myself.'

So Emily Guinea-Pig went first, her bag in her paw, and, resolutely smiling, was pulled

across the stormy void to safety. The Captain made haste to be next, and one by one the crew followed. Only the Weasel stayed on, for it had occurred to him that rockets in their present predicament might be very useful.

'Haul away, Tiffy!'

'Aye aye, sir –'

Crate after crate was swung ashore, while waves pounded the wreck to smithereens, and swept it away – and nearly swept the Weasel off as well. He had to leave in a hurry.

They were all rescued. Tiffy had saved them.

'Well done, young un',' said the Captain, thumping his Cabin-boy on the back. 'I'll see you get promotion for this. I'll make you a Captain. No, not a Captain, perhaps – Third Mate. Come on, you fellows, give him a cheer.'

The Rabbits cheered excitedly.

'You were very brave,' Emily told him. 'You set an example.'

The Weasel said nothing – he just gave Tiffy a certain sort of nod; Tiffy was pleased.

They collected a great pile of driftwood and made a bonfire; and when the flames leapt up, crackling and blazing, the gloomy morning seemed less gloomy, and that unknown foreign shore not so forbidding after all. Emily opened her bag. She got out her methylated spirits and her lamp, a tin of biscuits, a tin of milk, sugar, matches and tea. The kettle was filled with fresh water from a convenient spring. It was still raining, and their future was very uncertain, but there was much to be thankful for. Emily's kettle blew its whistle.

'Tea's ready,' she called. The crew stampeded. 'Two biscuits each, and one lump of sugar. You've taken seven lumps,' she said to the Captain, who had scooped his paw in the sugar-bowl.

'Yes, but look here – I'm the Captain – '

'You are not the Captain of my sugar,' Emily answered firmly; and she made him give it back. He was rather offended.

They sat in a circle round the fire, sipping hot tea and blowing biscuit crumbs at one another. Their fur dried, and their spirits revived.

'There's nothing like a nice cup of tea,' said Emily, contentedly.

'Except another,' said the Weasel, passing his empty coconut-shell.

When evening came, the storm was over.

The clouds had rolled away, and the sea was flat again, and their island, which had been simply grey when first seen, now turned wonderfully green and gold in the sunshine.

'Goodness, what a pretty place. Look at the flowers! I'm sure we shall manage,' said Emily.

She and Tiffy the Water Rat and the Weasel sat together under the palm-trees, discussing their situation. The Rabbits were playing hopscotch along the beach. The Captain was pacing slowly up and down beside the small exhausted waves.

'I am a Hare!' they heard him loudly reciting. 'I do! I dare! –'

'We're all right for food,' said the Water Rat. 'I been having a look round. There's bananas and coconuts in plenty, and grass for those as like it –'

'There's eggs, too,' said the Weasel. He was lying flat on his back, gazing up at the blue sky above. 'Any amount. The sand's full of 'em.'

'Eggs in the sand?' said Emily.

'Turtles eggs – that's what turtles do – bury their eggs in the sand, and I dare say they forget all about 'em, after,' said the Weasel, carelessly. 'They taste prime,' he added.

'But I don't think we ought to *take* their eggs – not without asking the turtles first,' said Emily. 'Perhaps we could come to some arrangement –'

'All right – you arrange it,' said the Weasel, rolling over to hide a grin. 'What about rescue? Any ideas?'

'I know what we ought to do,' said Tiffy. 'We ought to write a letter, and put it in a bottle, and throw the bottle in the sea. And we can let those rockets off, too.'

'We must keep the fire going,' said Emily, 'night and day – so that a passing ship can see the smoke, if it's in the daytime, or the flames if it's during the night.'

'Ah – but suppose no ship happens to be passing?' said the Weasel.

Emily bowed her head. A dreadful thought had come to her: supposing no ship ever passed again? – then she would never again see her home. Never! She felt quite faint, and reached for the sal volatile. And Arthur, who must be missing her already – how could he do without her, year after year, for ever? What about his socks?

'In my opinion,' the Weasel was saying, 'we'd do best with a bird. I've always found birds to be very reliable in the matter of messages – so long as it's the right sort of bird, of course. I'll see what I can do about it tomorrow.'

He got up and strolled off, and Tiffy went too, and Emily was left by herself. The sun dropped below the horizon, and at once it

was night. She lit her lantern, and opening her umbrella, established it on the soft sand under a palm tree. This was to be her shelter; she had often slept underneath her umbrella during her travels. Over the gap in front she draped her rug. Then Emily got her diary, and leaning back against her bag, she began to write. This is what she wrote in her diary:

'We have been shipwrecked – such a Mercy we were not all drowned. We owe our lives to W.R. – his courage an inspiration, and so young *too. Bananas etc. plentiful on this island – we shall not go hungry.*

There is indeed much to be thankful for, I have my Bag and Umbrella –'

She counted her blessings, and they were many, but oh! how far away was home, and she might never see it again. Never! the waves whispered from the beach, in the darkness. Emily put away her diary, and crawled inside her umbrella-tent, and hid her anxious thoughts in sleep.

Chapter Seven

Emily emerged from the greenish gloom of her umbrella, and stood blinking. How bright it was! The sunshine dazzled her. She was aware of blue sea, and blue sky, and of soft warm sand, and a smell of burning wood. Someone had stirred up the fire and put her kettle on top; perhaps the Weasel, though he was nowhere about.

'So this is what it's like,' she thought, 'to wake up on a desert island. Why, there's Tiffy – whatever is he doing?'

She shaded her eyes. Tiffy was hunting along the water's edge for pieces of wreckage. She watched him splashing in and out of the sea, pouncing and dragging. The sea sparkled; the splashes flew up, silver, round him. But the Captain sat on a rock, apart, his shoulders hunched and his ears drooping.

'Good morning, Captain,' she called out.

'I didn't sleep a wink,' he answered bitterly. 'How could I? There's no beds in this place – nothing! Not even a roof for the Captain's head.'

Emily felt sorry for him. She had been near to despair herself the night before, only this morning the sun was shining. And the slow sound of the waves reassured her: splosh, pause, splosh, pause. Arthur would come, they seemed to say to her; presently; splosh, pause – all in good time. She offered to lend the Captain her hammock.

'I don't at all mind sleeping on the sand – indeed, I find it very comfortable.'

The Captain cheered up at once. 'A hammock, eh? I didn't know you'd got one. You might have told me sooner.'

'Oh, I should never think of travelling

74

without a hammock,' said Emily. 'Travellers can never tell where they may have to put up for the night – they have to be prepared, you know, for anywhere.'

The Weasel reappeared for breakfast. He said he had been exploring. He ate his bananas and drank his tea with an abstracted air, and as soon as breakfast was over, he took the Water Rat and Emily aside.

'We're not the only ones on this island,' he told them. 'There's others.'

Emily was startled. 'What sort of others?'

'Monkeys and parrots, scores of 'em. They didn't see me.'

'Are they friendly?' she asked.

'That's what we've got to find out,' said the Weasel.

They left the beach behind them, and struck off into dense tropical vegetation. Everywhere creepers climbed and twisted. The light that filtered down through layers of leaves was dim and green, like the light under Emily's green umbrella. Long before they arrived at a clearing, they could hear chattering and squawking; but when they reached the edge of the clearing, they stood in doubt, for although the flickering sun and shade were full of voices, shrill, incessant, they could see no one.

'They're brown and green, same as the trees – that's why,' the Weasel whispered.

'We ought to introduce ourselves,' said Emily. 'What would be the best way, do you think?'

'Just walk out, I reckon, and leave it to them.'

They stepped forward. The squawking and chattering stopped at once. There was complete silence. Emily could tell they were being watched from every tree.

'How do you do?' she called – for she felt obliged to speak, to say at least something.

'I am Emily Guinea-Pig. These are my friends. Most unfortunately, we have been shipwrecked. I don't think they understand,' she said to the Weasel.

But suddenly there was a rush of movement, and they were surrounded by Monkeys and Parrots, all talking in a language that was incomprehensible; all except for one, their chief, a very old Monkey, very wrinkled, whose enigmatic eyes seemed to Emily to be full of wisdom and melancholy, as though he knew the answer to everything. He said nothing.

'I don't reckon conversation's any use,' Tiffy declared. 'We'd do better to have a sing-song.'

He sat down and crossed his legs and played a tune on his mouth-organ. The Parrots cocked their heads appreciatively, and when the Weasel whistled the tune, they whistled it too. The Weasel danced a horn-

pipe; in a trice all the Monkeys were dancing hornpipes with him. Dancing, whistling, flapping, screeching, the whole company set off towards the beach.

That morning the crew had overslept. As they sat outside their newly-dug burrows, sunning themselves and yawning, they heard the hullabaloo of the mob approaching through the jungle. Without hesitation, every Rabbit dived for safety, underground; so when Monkeys and Parrots flocked out from the trees on to the shore, only the Captain was there. Roused from a dream of glory, he snatched up the nearest weapon – Emily's green umbrella.

'Keep off!' he cried. 'Stand back, I say!'

'They are friends, Captain,' Emily bawled above the hubbub, ' – all friends!'

The Captain was much relieved. 'Oh, are they? Oh, good – can't have too many friends.' He went round from burrow to burrow, shouting down: 'Nothing to be afraid of – they won't hurt you. They haven't hurt me.'

One by one the crew ventured out, and made acquaintance. They had never seen Monkeys before; the Monkeys had never seen

Rabbits. They found each other most interesting. Soon they were all playing rounders together on the beach.

It was evening. Everyone was occupied. Tiffy was constructing a tent for the Captain from a torn sail and a spar and a couple of oars, and other bits of the wreckage he had salvaged.

'Make it big,' the Captain told him. 'Big enough for *me*, you know. You'd better measure my ears. I'm not like these other fellows – I need plenty of space. There's got to be plenty of room for me.'

'We've only the one sail, don't forget,' said Tiffy.

'Well, find another,' said the Captain. 'There must be lots of 'em floating about. Find 'em!'

'Yessir!'

Emily was sketching. The old monkey chief sat perfectly still under a coconut palm,

while Emily drew him. He stared past her at
the blue distance, at nothing.

'What can he be thinking?' she wondered.
'I wish I knew. I wish I could tell him of
Arthur and home. If only we could speak to
one another.'

The old chief sat without stirring, and his
thoughts were a secret Emily could never
share. Her own ran on like this:

'What a noise those animals make. I can

hardly hear the waves any more. Oh dear, now I've done his ear wrong.' She used her rubber. 'Now I've made a hole.'

She put her sketch down, and watched the Rabbits and Monkeys, who were running races. Some were playing leapfrog. Parrots were everywhere. A crowd of them perched on the top of her green umbrella, which the Captain held above his head as he paced up and down, reciting verses of his favourite poetry.

'He really mustn't borrow my things without asking. I shall have to speak about it. Goodness, what a noise!' she thought, dreamily. 'And all those young creatures growing up as wild as can be. I don't suppose they can any one of them read or write,' she said aloud, forgetting that her old companion would not understand her. But when she looked round, he had gone.

And a moment later the Parrots and

Monkeys went by with a scamper of feet and a rush of wings, and vanished into the jungle. The sun had touched the sea's horizon: day was over. The beach was deserted. Once again Emily heard the leisurely sound of the waves.

Tiffy threw himself down on the sand beside her. He had brought back her green umbrella, rather the worse for wear. It was going to need a stitch or two, Emily saw in dismay. And there and then she wrote out a label, and tied it to the handle:

'*Anyone taking this Property in Future will be REPRIMANDED.*'

'I've fixed the Skipper up some first-rate quarters,' said Tiffy. 'He's that pleased. He said he'd give me his autograph. I don't know what an autograph is, do you?'

But Emily was not listening. She had several problems on her mind. 'I can't make those turtles understand we mean to pay for their eggs. I've tried to give them money, but they simply walk away.'

Tiffy was not listening either. 'I reckon I could make myself a raft,' he said, 'or a boat, maybe – then I could go fishing. I could take you for a trip round the bay – you'd like that. There's all sorts of stuff washed up – planks and rigging – if only I had a saw. That's what I need. I might find one, tomorrow.'

'Tomorrow,' said Emily, 'I'm going to start a school.'

Just before darkness fell, they saw the Weasel, far out on a point of rock. He was absorbed in conversation with a seagull.

'*This is a Volcanic island*'

Emily wrote in her diary that night.

'*W. told me so, but he says the Volcano is Extinct – such a Disappointment. I have always so much wanted to see a real Volcano.*'

Chapter Eight

Arthur meant to be snug this winter. So long as there was plenty of grub, and he was warm enough, and never had to stick his nose out of doors, winter was all right, Arthur reckoned; and he made his plans accordingly.

First, he fetched his bed from upstairs, and got it into the kitchen. Carrie helped him, but with some reluctance. She was the Squirrel who came in to cook and clean and keep house for Arthur whenever Emily went off on her travels.

'I don't know what your sister would say, I'm sure.'

'Oh, don't you?' said Arthur, heaving his bed into place and lying down with a sigh of satisfaction. 'I do,' he said.

'Sleeping in the kitchen – she'd never approve.'

'What Emily don't see, Emily don't nag over,' Arthur answered. 'And don't you start fussing at me, Carrie, about what I mustn't do, or I'll tell Emily when she gets back to have a look under the carpets.'

This was where Carrie swept the dirt; it saved the nuisance of a dustpan. Arthur thought it was a very good idea; but Emily, they both knew, would think differently.

'You tell on me,' said Arthur, nodding at Carrie, 'and I'll tell on you.'

He made her giggle. Carrie considered Arthur very bold and amusing.

'As a matter of fact,' Arthur went on, 'you might as well give over cleaning the house while Emily's away. I've always felt it was a waste of time. Whatever you clean up one day, it's quite as bad again the day after, so where's the point? We'll have a bit of a tidy just before she gets back. I only hope she remembers to send us a postcard for warning this time. But there's no need to worry yet – we've got weeks and weeks to be comfortable in. So all you've got to do, Carrie, is to cook – d'you see? – and perhaps you'd better wash up too, because there's nothing so aggravating as washing-up when it isn't done.'

As soon as the news got round that Arthur was alone, his friends came visiting, and

Carrie was kept busy providing for the company who crammed into Emily's kitchen. All day long the kettle simmered on the stove, ready for their favourite brew of black-currant syrup in boiling water.

'It's good for coughs,' said Arthur, 'and we've all got coughs. Give us another dose, Carrie.'

They passed their mugs again and again.

And they were always hungry. All day long a stew-pot simmered beside the kettle. Carrie baked them bread and biscuits. She made fruit-cake and sponge-cake and seed-cake and doughnuts. They particularly liked her doughnuts.

'Put in plenty of *raspberry* jam, Carrie –'

All day long and half of the night, Carrie stirred and beat and mixed and poured. The air was thick with tobacco smoke. The talk and laughter never diminished. No one thought of going home to sleep. They dozed off on Arthur's bed, or on the floor, and woke at all hours to call for breakfast:

'Boiled eggs, Carrie – two apiece, mind!'

It was lucky Emily had preserved so many eggs last summer.

Only one creature was uneasy. He was a Mole, a close neighbour, Arthur's best friend. The notion that Emily might turn up at any time, any day, tormented him.

'What are you doing, Gregory? I never knew an animal so restless. Come away from the window, do.'

But Gregory rubbed at the steamy glass and peered towards the garden gate in fearful expectation.

'I think I maybe ought to be off now, Arthur.'

'Don't you be so foolish, Greg – it's raining out there. You'd get wet. You'd much better stop.'

'Well, I don't know – perhaps I will. It is

getting a bit darkish – she wouldn't travel by night, I don't suppose, would she?'

'Course not – pull up – have another mug o' grog. Give us a song, Carrie –'

Emily's kitchen was an unusually merry place that winter.

The fire had been a problem at first. Arthur loved a big fire, but he did not love at all having to fetch the wood to keep it burning. He hated going outside in winter. So what was he to do? Then two Dormice, twin brothers, arrived in search of lodgings, and Arthur had a brainwave: he said he would trade them lodgings for labour.

'You can stay all winter,' he told them, 'just so long as you never let the fire go out. If the fire goes out, then out you go – that's fair enough, it seems to me. You can have Emily's room to tuck up in, and I tell you what, you can have her alarm clock, to make sure you wake regular.'

The Dormice agreed, and took it in turns to wake, one in the morning, one in the evening, so that twice a day the kitchen crowd was disturbed by a sleepy Dormouse stumbling in with his load of logs and sticks.

Sometimes Gregory's voice would be heard: 'I wonder where Emily's got to now –'

And Arthur would hastily reply: 'She's all right, wherever she is. She's all right, and we're all right, so don't you fuss, Greg – enjoy yourself.'

But Gregory was never quite able to enjoy himself.

And then one night, very late, there came a knocking at the front door, a tapping and scratching. When Arthur opened the door, he found in the porch the same two Brown Owls who had come for Emily weeks before and he knew at once that something was wrong.

'What do you want?' he said. 'What is it?'

The Brown Owls answered nothing; only the first one opened his hooked beak, and let drop a scrap of paper. Arthur watched it flutter to the ground. Was it really for him? And must he read it? He had a foreboding that this bit of paper was going to spoil everything. Slowly he stooped and picked it up, and slowly went indoors.

'Well?' they all said, staring round at him, waiting.

Arthur unfolded the paper. It was a page from Emily's diary. He read aloud the words written on it, in Emily's tidy writing.

'We have been shipwrecked. Nobody drowned, but tea supplies low.'

Underneath the Weasel had pencilled in the latitude and longitude of their island.

'I knew it was bound to turn out badly,' said Arthur. 'I'm sorry, of course, but what's the use of telling me?'

'She means, you've got to rescue them,' said Gregory.

'What – *me?*' said Arthur.

'That's what she means,' said Gregory.

'But I've never rescued anyone in my life,' said Arthur. 'I don't know how to do it.'

Again they heard the scratching at the door.

93

'They're waiting to take you,' whispered Gregory.

Arthur knew he had to go. He had to leave his nice bed and his fire and his friends and his hot grog – he, who had never travelled, nor wanted to. But Emily was his sister, and he was fond of her, even if he did enjoy himself most when she was away.

He took a bag of doughnuts and drained his mug and went outside. How dark it was, and cold! He should have worn his mac at least – and what about a scarf for his chest? Too late! He felt himself seized – the black night wind whistled round his ears, and Arthur, all unready, was carried off.

He went to sleep. It was the only way he could manage to forget the unpleasantness of his situation. He stayed asleep, dreaming of home comforts, until the dangerous starry flight was over, and the Brown Owl dropped him on to a cold stone quay just as dawn was breaking.

Everything he saw was grey. He supposed that all that grey water slopping around down there must be the sea that Emily thought so much of. A large grey Gull with yellow eyes stood on one leg near by. It was the only creature, apart from himself, in sight. The two Brown Owls had disappeared, gone with the night.

Arthur sat down. He took a doughnut out of his bag and counted how many were left: five. Not many, he thought – not enough. The Gull had hopped nearer, hoping perhaps, for conversation; Arthur obliged.

'Rum sort of place, this,' he said, munching away. 'Lucky I thought of bringing my breakfast with me. Beats me what my sister sees in a place like this. I don't understand travel, never have – what's the point of being uncomfortable and wearing yourself out when you don't have to? And all this got-to-be-off stuff – well, I mean, I ask you, what comes of it?'

'Shipwreck,' said the Seagull, briefly.

Arthur was considerably surprised. 'Oh,' he said, 'so you know about that, do you?'

The Seagull put his head on one side, and looked sharply at Arthur's paper bag.

'I had a letter from Emily – ' Arthur began.

'I know you did,' said the grey Gull, and hopped closer. 'I brought it.'

'Oh, did you?' said Arthur. 'Oh well – in that case, I suppose – would you like a doughnut?'

'You bet!' said the Seagull. He opened his long yellow beak wide and the fifth doughnut was gone in a single gulp.

There was silence for a while.

'What does she expect me to do?' said Arthur presently. 'I mean, how can I rescue her – me? I can't fly. I can't swim. I'm not used to travel.'

'I'll fix it,' said the Gull, and it spread its narrow wings and swooped away.

'What a lot of slang that fellow does talk,' said Arthur to himself. ' "I'll fix it!" "You bet!" Of course when you travel about you hear this sort of foreign lingo – bound to. Perhaps I'll just have another bite, while he's gone. That'll fix it! Ha ha! You bet!'

The Seagull returned, perched on the funnel of a tug. At the wheel of the tug stood an old grey Otter.

'He'll take you to Emily,' screeched the Seagull. With a yell of laughter, it dived at Arthur, and snatched the paper bag from his paw, and soared up, up. The paper tore; the doughnuts fell – one in the sea, and two on the deck of the tug. Arthur scrambled aboard, most indignant.

'That bird – he's a hooligan!'

'Oh, he don't mean no harm,' said the old
Otter, calmly. 'High spirits, that's all it is.
You mustn't mind him. See how he pick that
bun out of the water? – I couldn't have done
it neater myself, given I had wings. There's
no birds like Gulls for flying, to my mind –
beautiful to watch, they are, pretty as ships.
Air-sailors, we call 'em. See how he beat up
against the wind and then come slipping
away sideways down the current? – you
can't do that with sails and sea half so well
as you can do it with wings and air. But it's
blowy up there – tends to make them high-

spirited. They don't mean no harm – they're just naturally frolicsome, Gulls are.'

Arthur retrieved his last two doughnuts. He offered one to the old grey Otter. He felt he had to.

'Thank you kindly – I won't say no. And very nice too. I understand it's your sister as we're going after? Ah! – I heard of her. Took passage with that Hare, and a prime piece of folly it were to ship along o' he – ain't no creature under the sun knows less about sailing than that Hare, except maybe his crew. Mind, he's got a Cabin-boy as good a little old sailor as ever was. Born to the water, same as myself. Your sister, now – she wouldn't be a water animal, would she?'

'Emily's never been to sea before,' said Arthur. 'But she's a traveller, and I daresay you know what travellers are like – they get a feeling they have to be off, and off they go. Now that's not like me – I never want to be off – *never!*' said Arthur, with all his heart and soul, and at this moment he began to feel sick.

The rest of the voyage he knew nothing about. He crawled underneath a tarpaulin and went firmly to sleep. His dreams protected him from hunger and sickness and every other trouble, and time passed, days and nights, and nights and days, and hundreds of miles of ocean and a storm or two, and Arthur knew nothing of any such things, until he heard the old Otter say:

'Right ahead, it's bound to be, according to my calculations.'

Arthur emerged into a night as warm as a summer's afternoon.

'Have we got there? I don't see an island. Where is it?'

But even as he spoke a rocket went careering up amongst the stars, and paused, and exploded, and flung out a cascade of different, falling, fading stars; and another rocket followed, and then a third.

'Seems like as though we might be expected,' the old Otter remarked.

Chapter Nine

Weeks and weeks had passed. Emily sat in the shade of her green umbrella and wondered how much longer it would be before Arthur came. Supposing their message had gone astray? Or supposing Arthur, setting out to rescue them, had taken a wrong direction? She never doubted that he had set out; only – how long must they wait? More and more she thought of home; every day it seemed to her more dear and farther off, and every day her desire to spring-clean grew stronger.

Nobody else was homesick. The others by this time had ceased to care a button whether they were ever rescued or not. Life was extremely pleasant and easy: the sand was always warm, and food plentiful; work was not essential. So why bother to keep a watch for passing ships? Why bother with smoke signals by day, and rockets by night? Why bother? Why worry? said the Rabbits. They broke open a packing-case and set up shop in safety-pins.

'Enterprising fellows,' said the Captain, strolling by. Parrots surrounded him, wherever he went. 'Good luck to 'em, I say – don't you agree, Miss Pig?'

'Good luck!' squawked the Parrots, 'good luck! – good luck!'

'I'm not so sure,' answered Emily, doubtingly. 'Those Monkeys don't seem to know what safety-pins are for –'

They had decorated their trees with long silvery chains of safety-pins, looped from branch to branch, so that the trees themselves seemed to sparkle and flash in the sunshine, and tinkle when the wind blew.

'It isn't what *for* that counts in trade – it's how much,' said the Captain. 'Mind you, I'm not a trader myself, but I take an interest. School going well?' he went on, hoping the topic might cheer Emily up, for he could see that she was in the doldrums.

But Emily was not sure about her school either. She looked down at the lively young Monkeys, her pupils, turning somersaults on the beach below, and she sighed.

'They know their A B C and one two three,' she told him.

'Do they? Well done! – splendid!'

'But it isn't enough,' said Emily.

'Never mind about enough,' the Captain cried. 'It's the beginning that counts. To start – to set off – that's the thing! Who cares for Z and twenty? – it's A B C and number one that matter!'

'I am a Hare,' squawked the Parrots, much excited, flying about his ears. 'I am a Hare, a Hare! Good luck!'

'He isn't right,' said Emily to herself, as she watched him saunter off, with the bright birds round him. 'Ends do matter as well as beginnings. And oh dear! – *why* doesn't Arthur come? I've only got a spoonful of tea left.'

That night she wrote in her diary:

'*I know it is wrong of me to feel so Low, but I do want to go Home, and I wish Arthur would hurry. Where can he be?*'

Chapter Ten

It was night, but Emily could not sleep. She stood alone on the glimmering shore and stared out across the water. Arthur was near: she knew it.

Alone she climbed the jungly slope and heard the Parrots and Monkeys stir in their sleep and rustle the leaves of the dark branches over her head. The dangling chains of safety-pins tinkled as she blundered past. Creepers caught at her legs. Emily forced her way on – Arthur was near, and she must direct him.

She left the trees and ascended, puffing, the steep side of the hill that had once been a volcano, until she reached its bare and rocky summit. There below her lay the entire island, with its slumbering jungle, its circle of pale beaches, the beaches circled by white waves, and around, for miles, the black and silver sea.

Emily took a rocket from the crate that stood ready, and fixed it pointing at the sky, and lit the blue paper. With a fizz and a whizz, the rocket shot away. She lit another, and another, and watched them bursting into showers of coloured lights. And then, far out in the path of the moon, she saw the shape of a vessel, and knew that Arthur had indeed come at last.

'At last!' said Emily.

Down she scrambled, slipping, rolling over in her haste, calling aloud:

'He's come, he's come – Arthur's here!'

Every bird and animal awoke and flocked to the beach.

'He's come!' screeched the Parrots. 'Arthur's here! – Arthur's here!'

Nobody knew who Arthur was. The crew, greatly agitated, began to dig new burrows.

But the Monkeys were jubilant. They made a bonfire, and danced round it, chanting for joy:

'Is *com* arthursere! – is *com* arthursere!'

Arthur was gratified to be met by such a large crowd. He realized as he stepped ashore that he must be a hero.

Emily embraced her brother. 'I knew you'd come,' she said, proudly.

'Well, of course,' said Arthur, patting her shoulder. 'How are you, my dear? Good of you to write. I'm afraid I forgot to bring the tea.'

'Never mind,' said Emily. 'We shall soon be home. Oh, Captain – I want you to meet my brother.'

'Delighted,' said the Captain, bowing. 'A pleasant trip, I trust – no storms? I see you use an engine. Most ingenious – as a matter of fact, I've been meaning to try an engine myself.'

Arthur thought him very civil. 'Nice chap,' he said to Emily.

The old Otter remained on board his tug. He said he was better off with a drop of water underneath him; and he went below for a nap. But no one else wanted to sleep – they wanted to celebrate.

The celebrations went on for hours. Up and down the luminous beach the dark figures capered, letting off fireworks, especially squibs, and the sharp smell of gunpowder blew in the wind, with the smell and the smoke of burning driftwood, and tickled Arthur's nose, and made him sneeze.

Arthur enjoyed himself immensely. There was plenty to eat and plenty to drink and everyone dropped their banana skins on the ground and he was the guest of honour: it was an ideal party. And when the festive night was over, and the fire was in ashes, and the sun rose, and the sky was blue, and Emily said it was time to go, Arthur was dismayed.

He liked this island.

He liked the soft sand, so comfortable for lying down on. He liked the ripe fruit that fell, ready for eating, out of the trees. He liked the sleepy splash of the waves, and the marvellous warm breezes. He loved the sunshine. But it was no good – Emily had packed her bag and folded her umbrella: she wanted to go home.

In her mind's eye she could see, waiting, her garden gate, her own front door.

'East, west, home's best,' she said.

'What about south?' mumbled Arthur, drowsily. He envied the Rabbits – they were staying. This was their home now. They had forgotten ever having had another.

And the Captain declared he must stop with his crew: it was his duty. He said he would take charge of Emily's school, and teach her pupils poetry.

'But they must learn arithmetic too,' said Emily. 'And reading and writing and history and grammar –'

But the Skipper replied that poetry was quite enough to learn on a desert island. He was not at all grateful when Emily gave him her hammock as a leaving present: he thought she had given, not lent it, already.

'I could do with your lantern,' he said. 'It's just what I need –'

Emily gave him her lantern.

'And how about your kettle, Miss Thingummy? – and that old rug of yours –'

'It's not old,' said Emily, huffily, 'and you can't have it – I've given it to another friend. No, Captain, nothing more. And be so kind as to remember that my name is Emily Guinea-Pig.'

He drew himself up; he was twice as tall as her, an imposing figure – 'Miss Emily Guinea-Pig, allow me to present myself: Admiral Hare – at your service, madam.'

'Oh, indeed?' said Emily.

He bowed. He blew his nose. 'A little matter of promotion – overdue.'

'I see. Congratulations. Good-bye, Captain.'

'Not Captain, Miss Pig – *Admiral!*'

Tiffy the Water Rat nearly decided to settle there too.

'You come aboard,' said the old Otter,

scandalized. 'The only rightful place for an animal born to the water is afloat – and if you do like I say, smart and lively, and I don't hear no more of this palm-tree talk, who knows but what this here craft mightn't be yours one of these days, when I come to retire.'

'Yessir!' cried Tiffy, full of shame and hope.

'Then stand by to cast off.'

The Weasel stepped lightly aboard, at the very last moment.

'I was afraid you were going to stay behind as well,' said Emily. She was glad to see him.

'I never stay,' said the Weasel.

They leaned on the rail together and looked back over the stern. The palm-trees dwindled. No one was waving, or taking any notice of their departure. Only above the sound of the surf, fainter and fainter, they heard the screech of Parrots:

'I am a Hare – !'

'They've forgotten us already,' said Emily.

'What was in that matchbox?' asked the Weasel.

Emily had once given the old chief of the Monkeys a box of matches, and when they parted he gave her back the box. He had used up all the matches, Emily knew.

'Nothing,' she said. 'But it's the thought that counts,' she added, rather severely, for she noticed the Weasel was grinning.

'Are you so sure it's empty?' he said.

Emily opened the matchbox. Inside, on a stuffing of dry grass, lay a huge pink pearl.

'Ah!' said the Weasel, softly, 'that's worth more than a thought, that is – I reckon that's worth a fortune.'

Emily had never been given such a present before. Her little eyes shone with joy. 'It's the thought,' she said again, 'that counts.'

Their return voyage was uneventful. Emily

was once more a passenger; she was not allowed to steer. She sat wrapped in her plaid overcoat, content to sniff the salty wind and know that every stroke of the engine carried her nearer home.

They reached the stone jetty one fine calm evening. A corked bottle was bobbing about at the foot of the steps. There was a message in it:

'Ship gone to bottom, crew ashore, requiring rescue.'

Tiffy had written the message. He put the bottle in his pocket – for a souvenir, he said.

Emily offered the Weasel hospitality. 'Arthur and I would be so pleased if you would care to spend a few days with us.'

'Spend a few weeks,' said Arthur.

But the Weasel declined. He said he had certain matters to attend to.

'Another time,' said he, and tipped his hat and strolled away into the dusk.

The old Otter and his new Cabin-boy had already chugged off. Arthur and Emily were left on their own. As they looked about uncertainly, two shadowy forms floated down from the darkening sky: the Brown Owls had come to fetch them home.

Very early next morning, before sunrise, Emily and her brother were set down beside their garden gate. Emily opened the gate, and went up the path. Green tips of daffodils showed above the brown earth: winter was over. She lifted the latch, and pushed open the front door, and stepped inside. An alarm clock was ringing loudly overhead, and a moment later two small sleepy animals came tumbling down the stairs.

'Is it spring?' they said to Emily.

'Yes, indeed!' she answered in amazement.

'We kep' it up,' they said to Arthur, 'all

winter, as agreed.' And then they scuttled out of the front door and away.

'But, Arthur,' said Emily, 'whoever were they?'

'They looked pretty much like Dormice to me,' said Arthur, evasively. He did hope his bed was not still in the kitchen. But no! – it had been returned to its proper place. The kitchen was quite as usual, except for quantities of firewood, stacked to the ceiling.

'You leave it to me,' said Arthur, relieved that all other signs of jollification had disappeared. 'I'll fix it! – you bet!'

Emily thought these expressions rather coarse. She was surprised to hear her brother use them.

'Oh, you're bound to pick up foreign talk when you travel around,' said Arthur. 'I daresay I'll pick up a good deal more next winter,' he added, with satisfaction.

'Next winter? – but you surely don't mean to go away again, Arthur? – you used to say you *never* wanted to go away.'

'It depends where you go away *to*,' said Arthur. 'That friend of yours – that Hare – he's invited me. I said I'd take him out a few things. He wants a carpet – and a flag – and some dominoes – he gave me a list. It's all arranged – I'm going by tug. I don't think this climate suits my chest in winter, Emily. And besides, a little travel does you good.'

Emily spent the day getting accustomed to her house again, trotting up and down the stairs, opening windows, opening drawers, peering into cupboards. There were no eggs left, she found, and the black-currant syrup was quite finished; so was the jam, and most of her other stores too. She was thankful to know that Arthur had not lost his appetite during her absence, though sorry to think what a bad cough he must have had. But the sight of her empty shelves gave Emily much satisfaction. How busy the summer was going to be, bottling, preserving – she was delighted: so much to do!

One discovery pleased her considerably less: the sheets on her bed were *not clean*. She went outside and told Arthur, who was resting on a flower-pot.

'What can have been happening here while we've been away?' she said. 'It's very strange, don't you think?'

'Very rum indeed,' said Arthur.

He was tired. Clearing the wood from the

kitchen had been hard work. That night he
went to bed early.

But Emily sat up late, alone, and looked
at her pink pearl. Once more she heard the
rattle of palm-tree leaves in a hot breeze; the
splosh and sigh of tropical surf; the creak of
rigging, the whine of a rising gale. When she
shut her eyes she saw the green Parrots
flashing out of the jungle, and Monkeys sil-
houetted against the glinting sea, and the slow
turtles lumbering off across the white sand.

Emily opened her eyes: she was not there — she was here. In her pocket was a piece of coral. She put it on the window-sill amongst her potted geraniums. The room was very quiet. Its only sound was the tick of the clock.

Emily unfastened her battered bag, and got out her diary. This is what she wrote in it:

'I am so very glad to be Back. There is NO PLACE like Home.'

Travellers love to travel; but what they love best of all is coming home again, afterwards.

We hope you have enjoyed this book.
There are many more Young Puffins
to choose from, and some of them
are described on the following pages.

Bel the Giant and Other Stories
Helen Clare

More imaginative and charming stories for four and
five year olds, told by the author of *Five Dolls in a House*.

The Dolls' House
Rumer Godden

Mr and Mrs Plantaganet and their family were very
happy in their antique doll's house, until Marchpane the
elegant, selfish china doll moved in with them and acted
as if she owned the place.

How the Whale Became
Ted Hughes

Eleven stories, beautifully told by one of our leading
younger poets.

Albert
Alison Jezard

The adventures of a nice cheerful bachelor bear who
lives in the East End of London.

Dear Teddy Robinson
More About Teddy Robinson
Joan G. Robinson

Teddy Robinson was Deborah's teddy bear and such
a very nice, friendly, cuddly bear that he went
everywhere with her – and had even more
adventures than she did.

Flat Stanley
Jeff Brown and Tomi Ungerer

Stanley Lambchop was an ordinary boy, except for one thing – he was four feet tall, about a foot wide, and only half an inch thick!

The Ten Tales of Shellover
Ruth Ainsworth

Shellover the tortoise tells one story for each of the creatures in Mrs Candy's garden.

Robin
Catherine Storr

Robin was the youngest of three, and hated it. And then he discovered the shell called the Freedom of the Seas – and became the wonder of his family.

Miss Happiness and Miss Flower
Rumer Godden

Nona was lonely far away from her home in India, and the two dainty Japanese dolls, Miss Happiness and Miss Flower, were lonely too. But once Nona started building them a proper Japanese house they all felt better.

Magic in my Pocket
Alison Uttley

A selection of short stories by this well-loved author, especially good for five and six year olds.

The Secret Shoemakers
James Reeves

A dozen of Grimms' least-known fairy tales retold
with all a poet's magic, and illustrated sympathetically
by Edward Ardizzone.

Tales from the End Cottage
More Tales from the End Cottage
Eileen Bell

Two tabby cats and a Peke live with Mrs Apple in a
Northamptonshire cottage. They quarrel, have
adventures and entertain dangerous strangers. A new
author with a special talent for writing about animals.
For reading aloud to 5 and over, private reading 7
plus. (*Original*)

George
Agnes Sligh Turnbull

George was good at arithmetic, and housekeeping, and
at keeping children happy and well behaved. The pity
of it was that he was a rabbit so Mr Weaver didn't
believe in him. Splendid for six-year-olds and over.

The Young Puffin Book of Verse
Barbara Ireson

A deluge of poems about such fascinating subjects as
birds and balloons, mice and moonshine, farmers and
frogs, pigeons and pirates, especially chosen to please
young people of four to eight. (*Original*)

Clever Polly and the Stupid Wolf
Polly and the Wolf Again
Catherine Storr

Clever Polly manages to think of lots of good ideas to stop the stupid wolf from eating her.

Gobbolino, the Witch's Cat
Ursula Moray Williams

Gobbolino's mother was ashamed of him because his eyes were blue instead of green, and he wanted to be loved instead of learning spells. So he went in search of a friendly kitchen.

The Happy Orpheline
Natalie Savage Carlson

The twenty little orphaned girls who live with Madame Flattot are terrified of being adopted because they are so happy.

A Brother for the Orphelines
Natalie Savage Carson

Sequel to *The Happy Orpheline*. Josine, the smallest of all the orphans, finds a baby left on the doorstep. But he is a *boy*. So the orphans plot and worry to find a way to keep him.

A Gift From Winklesea
Helen Cresswell

Dan and Mary buy a beautiful stone like an egg as a present for their mother – and then it hatches out, into the oddest animal they ever saw.